Once upon a time there was a little farm in a corner of a small village.

On this little farm lived five friends:
Pig, Cow, Duck, Sheep, and Hen.

Duck

Sheep

Hen

The friends visited a pond near the forest to bathe every day. The pond was a bit far away from the farm and not very safe. It was rather deep for the animals that couldn't swim so well. And sometimes Fox would sneak by and steal clothes and soap from the animals while they were bathing.

"What if we made a bathtub?" Duck said one day while splashing in the pond.

"That's a good idea!" Cow said. "Let's make a huge bathtub!"

"I think there's wood and some other things we can use in the old barn," Sheep said.

So, they all went to the old barn and searched for the things they needed to make the bathtub.

"Hey! I found some wood," oinked Pig.

"I found some iron nails," clucked Hen.

"Here is a varnish tin," quacked Duck flapping her wings.

"Yay! I found a
hammer."
Cow jumped
for joy.

"I found a saw,
so, we can cut
the wood,"
said Sheep.

Everybody worked so hard making the bathtub. They were eager to try it out. But the varnish was still wet, so they had to wait until the next day.

They all took turns. Pig made up a special timetable so that the friends would know when it was their turn to use the bathtub.

Timetable

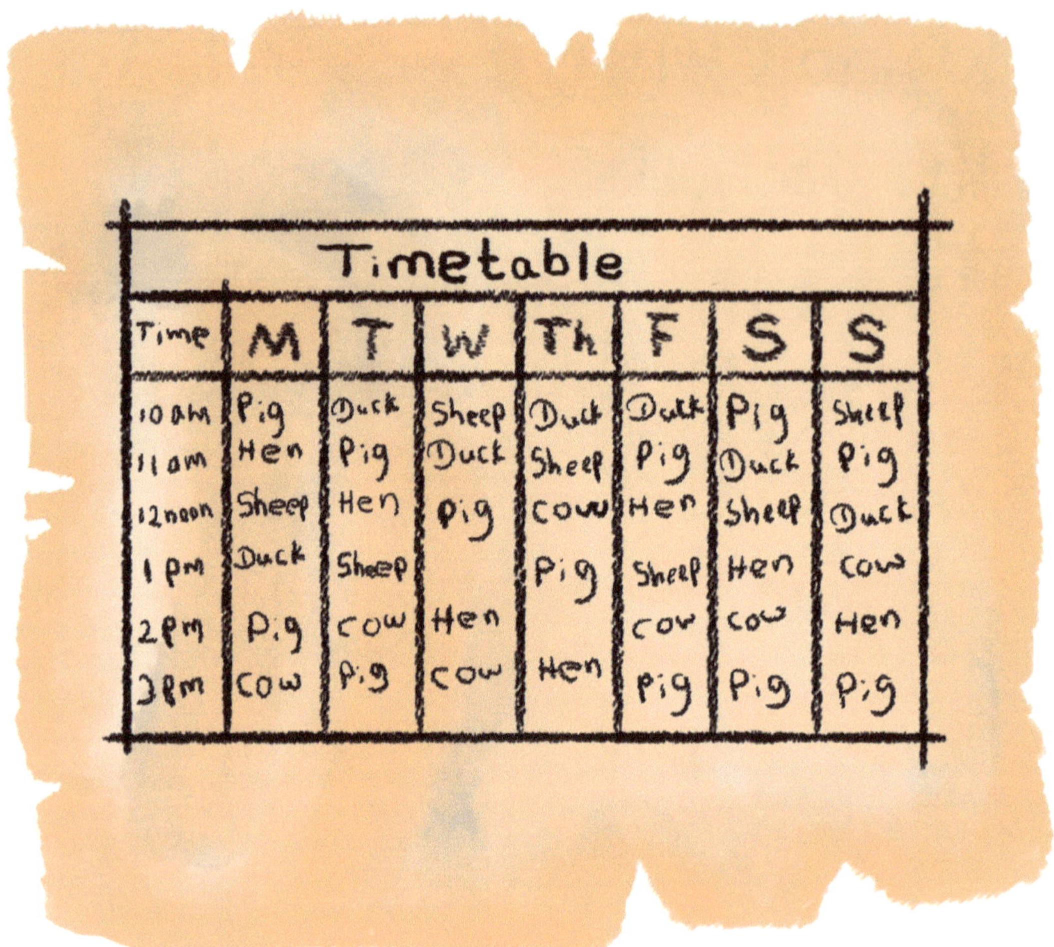

Time	M	T	W	Th	F	S	S
10am	Pig	Duck	Sheep	Duck	Duck	Pig	Sheep
11am	Hen	Pig	Duck	Sheep	Pig	Duck	Pig
12noon	Sheep	Hen	Pig	Cow	Hen	Sheep	Duck
1pm	Duck	Sheep		Pig	Sheep	Hen	Cow
2pm	Pig	Cow	Hen		Cow	Cow	Hen
3pm	Cow	Pig	Cow	Hen	Pig	Pig	Pig

The first few days everything went well. Then it all started to go wrong.

"Pig always chooses the best time to bathe and gives us the worst times," complained Hen.

"I want to baath when I want to baath. How can Pig decide when I should baath?" protested Sheep.

"Pig bathes for more than an hour. I have to wait forever until my turn comes," quacked Duck.

"I have lots of mud all over my body. I definitely need more time," oinked Pig.

Everybody tried to jump into the bathtub at the same time and made a terrible splash.

"What is that ugly noise?" Fox was passing the farm and stopped to take a look.

"Oh! A bathtub," said Fox.

Fox waited until everyone came dripping out from the bathtub, mooing, bleating, oinking, quacking, and clucking.

While they were arguing, Fox grabbed the bathtub and ran away.

"Look! The fox is stealing our bathtub."
screamed Hen. But it was too late.
Fox was faster than them.

Everybody was so sad. They all started crying.

"This was all my fault," oinked Pig with tears running down his snout.

"No, it was my fault. I started the fight," clucked Hen.

"No, it was all our faults. We never should have fought," said Cow.

Fox went home and boiled some water to have a nice hot bath. But he couldn't enjoy it because he could hear the cries of the farm animals.

Even after he'd finished his bath and gone to bed, Fox was still disturbed by the crying from the farmhouse.

"I'm done. I will return this bathtub in the morning," said Fox as he tried to sleep.

In the morning, Fox picked up the
bathtub and carried it back to the
farmhouse.

There he found Pig, Cow, Duck, Sheep
and Hen still wearing their bath caps
and towels and bawling loudly.

"I'm sorry. Here is your bathtub.
Please stop crying," said Fox.
Pig, Cow, Duck, Sheep and Hen were
so happy to get their bathtub back.

They thanked Fox and invited him to take a turn in the bathtub too.

Pig added him to the timetable and made sure that this time they ALL had equal turns.

Author and illustrator

Tina Wijesiri

Freelance illustrator and children's book writer

https://www.facebook.com/Cute-illustrations-334947500254178/

Editor

Debbie Manber Kupfer

debbiemanberkupfer.wordpress.com/editing-and-proofreading/